Waltham Forest Libraries

C

Please return this item by the last date stamped. The loan may be renewed unless required by another customer.

May 2014		

D1347017

Need to renew your books?
http://www.walthamforest.gov.uk/libraries or
Dial 0333 370 4700 for Callpoint – our 24/7 automated telephone renewal line. You will need your library card number and your PIN. If you do not know your PIN, contact your local library.

*"To Kavi, my sister and my
first kite-flying partner."*

- Chitra Soundar

Farmer Falgu Goes Kite Flying

Chitra Soundar

Kanika Nair

"A perfect day," said Farmer Falgu
as he cleaned his cart.

"For flying kites," said Eila, smiling.

"Let us get our kites," said Farmer Falgu.
"And go to the fairgrounds."

They loaded the bullock cart with a spool of thread,
four kites, some lunch, and a box of odds and ends.

"This one is mine," said Eila, holding up a kite.

The bells on the bullocks tinkled as
the wind blew softly.

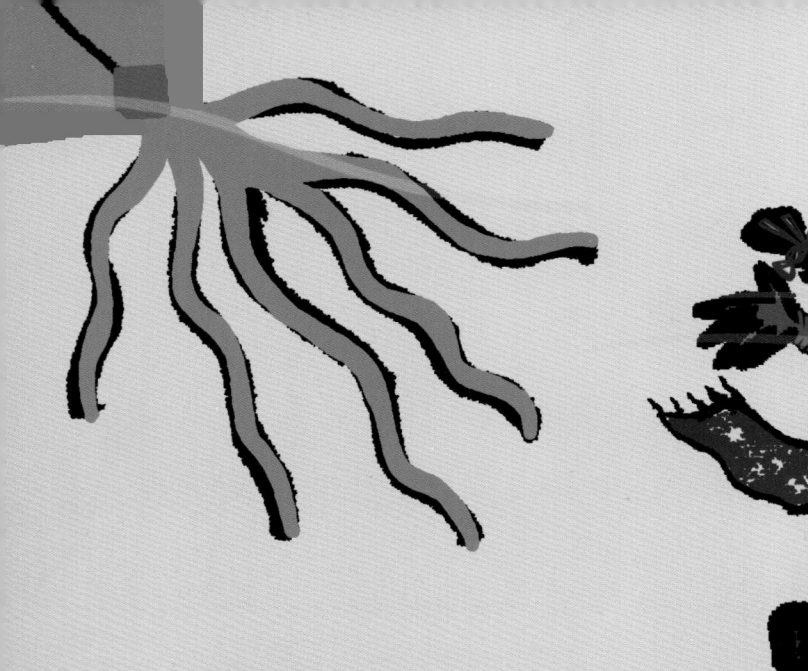

Suddenly,

WHOOOSH!

"Papa!" cried Eila.
"Catch my kite!"

The wind had carried
Eila's kite away.

Eila's face fell. She became quiet.

"Don't worry," said Farmer Falgu.
"Choose another one."

They continued on their journey as
the wind gathered speed.

The cart turned the corner of the sugarcane fields. "Falgu, stop!" called out Ahmed,
the balloon-man.

"Are you going to the fair?" asked Ahmed. "Could you please give me a lift?"

"Hop on!" said Farmer Falgu.

"I lost my kite to the wind, Ahmed Chacha," said Eila.

"You can always fly mine," said Ahmed, holding up his orange kite.

The wind blew stronger.

WHOOOSH!

"Catch my kite,"

cried Ahmed. "Oh! My balloons too!"

The wind now carried Ahmed's kite and balloons away.
They soon drifted out of sight.

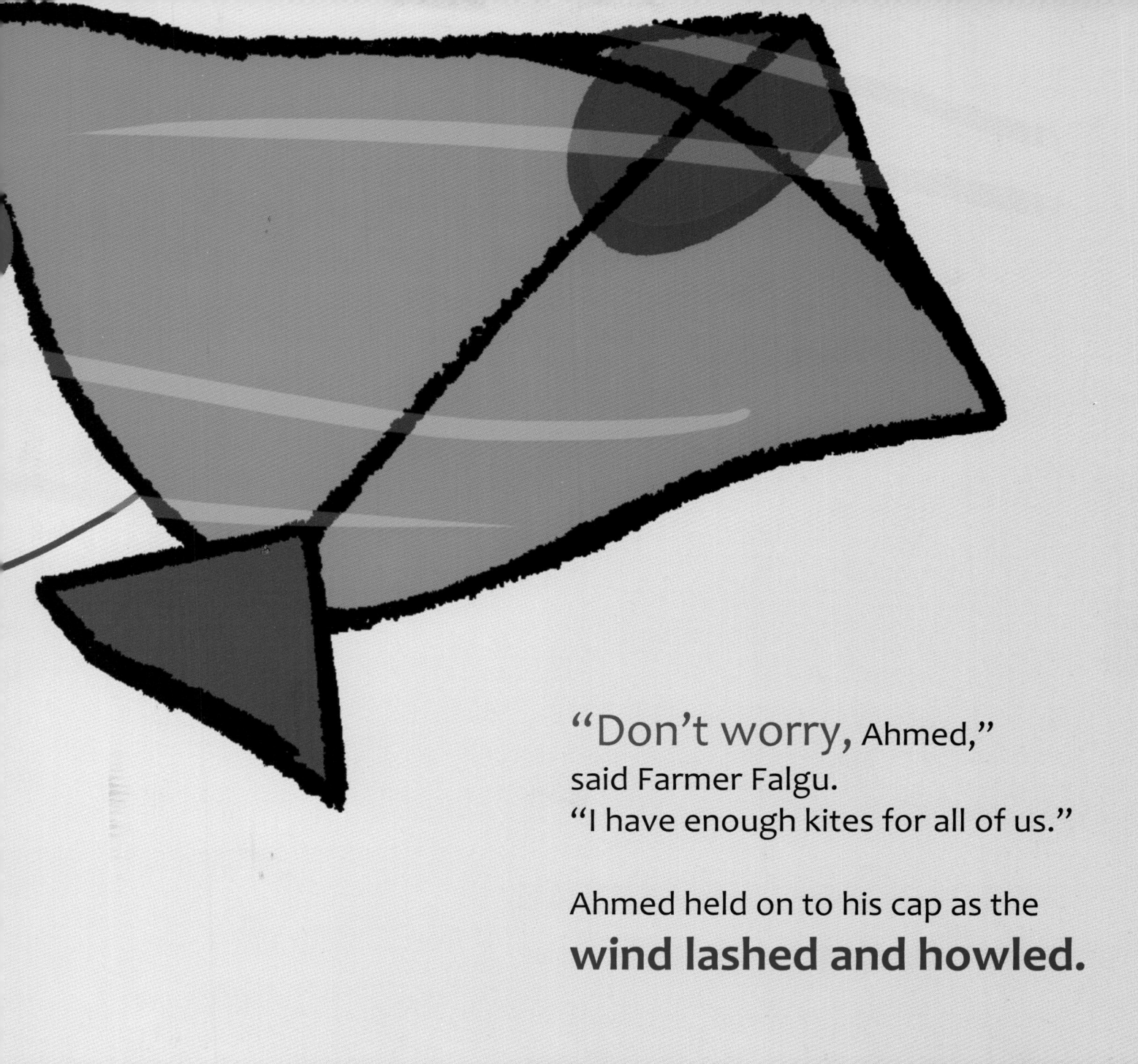

"Don't worry, Ahmed,"
said Farmer Falgu.
"I have enough kites for all of us."

Ahmed held on to his cap as the
wind lashed and howled.

Just as the bullock cart slowed down
for a herd of goats to pass, "Falgu Bhaiyya!"
called Pushpa, the fortune teller.

"Are you going to the fair to fly kites?"
asked Pushpa. "Can I come along?"

"Hop on!" said Farmer Falgu.

"Look, Eila!" said Pushpa, carefully
taking a kite out of her bag.

"It's beautiful, Pushpa Didi. But be careful,"
warned Eila. "The wind stole our kites!"

The bullock cart rattled as
the wind grew fierce.

BAAAAH!

WHOOOSH!

"Catch my kite!"
shouted Pushpa.

"Catch my kite!"
repeated her parrot.

But the wind had snatched
Pushpa's kite and flung it
far into the clouds!

"Don't worry, Pushpa Didi,"
said Eila. "We can spare you a kite.
Can't we, Papa?"

Farmer Falgu nodded.

By the time the bullocks waddled past millet farms and sunflower fields,

the wind was *raging.*

At the fairgrounds, people were **struggling** to hold on to their kites.

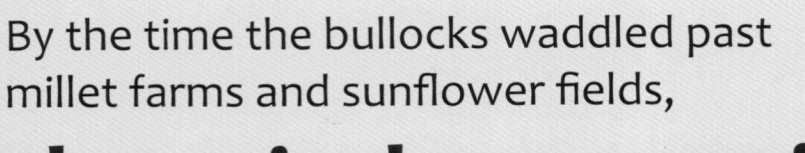

The bells on the bullocks clanged.

The parrot screeched.

Eila clutched her scarf.

Ahmed held on to his cap.

Pushpa tightened her saree around herself.

Farmer Falgu parked the bullock-cart and opened his bag.

The wind whipped

at his clothes.

"Oh no," cried Eila as
Farmer Falgu pulled out the remaining kites.

The kites were scrunched,
torn, and tattered.

There wasn't a single good kite
left for them to fly.

"Hai dahiya," mumbled Ahmed.

"Oiee maa," said Pushpa and sighed.

"Oiee maa," echoed the parrot.

"What are we going to do, Papa?" asked Eila, crying.

"Don't worry," said Farmer Falgu.

"Go get the broomstick, Eila.

Ahmed, get the box from the cart.

Pushpa, find me a pair of scissors."

Farmer Falgu then pulled the spool
of thread from his bag.

"We need a large colourful
piece of cloth," he said,
looking around.

"But we didn't bring any
cloth, Papa," said Eila.

"Aha!" said Farmer Falgu, unfurling his turban.

"Pushpa," he called. "Cut this into triangles.

Eila, give me the sticks from the broom."

Eila pulled out the sticks from the broom. Farmer Falgu tied them together tightly with the thread.

Ahmed helped Farmer Falgu drape the cloth over the frames and knot them together.

"All we need now are tails for the kite," said Eila, handing him the ribbons from her hair.

"Perfect!" said Farmer Falgu.

"Hold this carefully," said Farmer Falgu, handing the spool of thread to Eila. As he let go of the kite, Eila tugged at the thread.

WHOOOSH!

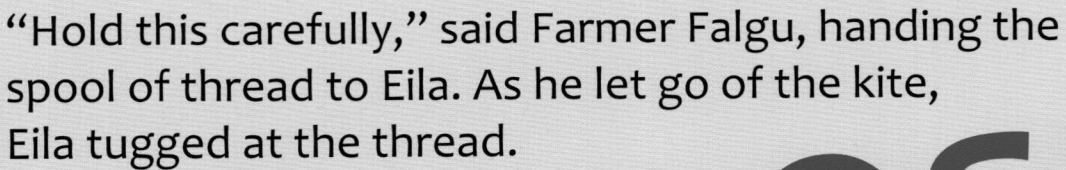

The kite rose majestically into the sky.
"It's four kites in one," shouted Eila.

"One for each of us," said Farmer Falgu, smiling at Ahmed and Pushpa.

Everyone cheered and clapped as the kite soared.

"Papa, our kite is the best in the sky!" gushed Eila.

The **gusty wind** was now a *gentle breeze* and it carried their new kite into the sky.

CHITRA SOUNDAR

Chitra hails from India, resides in London, and lives in imaginary worlds woven out of stories. She has written over twenty books for children. Chitra also loves to retell folktales, legends, and ancient tales from the Indian subcontinent. Though she dabbles in chapter books, her first love is picture books.

KANIKA NAIR

Kanika Nair has always had a passion for illustration. After receiving a bachelor's degree in communication design from Pearl Academy of Fashion, New Delhi, she began working as a freelance illustrator, writer, and designer of children's books. She loves to incorporate various insights about children that she has collected over the years into her illustrations. The Indian cultural canvas has always fascinated her, and this is evident in her artistic style.

About the Kite Festival

The Kite Festival in Rajasthan marks the start of spring, when the sun starts its journey away from the Tropic of Capricorn. Farmers across India also celebrate Makara Sankaranthi, the Harvest Festival, on this day.

In Rajasthan, the day is celebrated with an early morning dip in the river, a prayer to the Sun, and lots of good food and sweets. It is a day of family gatherings, friendly challenges, and kite flying. The bright and sunny sky is covered in colourful kites that are either homemade or bought from small local shops. People descend from all across the country and even the world to take part in kite-flying competitions.

The International Kite Festival runs from January 14 to January 16 every year, in Jaipur, the capital city of Rajasthan. If you love kites, why not visit and fly a kite? Who knows – you might meet Farmer Falgu too!

Farmer Falgu Goes Kite Flying

Text: Chitra Soundar
Illustrations: Kanika Nair

Second Reprint 2018

Karadi Tales Company Pvt. Ltd.
3A Dev Regency, 11 First Main Road,
Gandhinagar, Adyar, Chennai 600 020
Ph: +91 44 4205 4243
email: contact@karaditales.com
Website: www.karaditales.com

ISBN: 978-81-8190-356-3

The Farmer Falgu Series

Goes on a Trip

Goes to the Market

Goes to the Kumbh Mela